Papua, New Guinea, 1983

DELORES J. DILLARD

ISBN: Softcover   978-1-4535-3939-2
       EBook   978-1-4691-2468-1

Print information available on the last page

Rev. date: 04/03/2019

To order additional copies of this book, contact:
Xlibris
1-888-795-4274
www.Xlibris.com
Orders@Xlibris.com

INTRODUCTION

Delores Dillard is a dynamic African American on the cutting edge of ministry that crosses racial barriers and continents. She has been an active, working member of Good Samaritan Ministries both nationally and internationally. She trains counselors and ministers, for active field ministry locally in Oregon, but also, very significantly, in several countries in Africa.

In her new book, "***Papua, New Guinea 1983,***" *you get a new view and definition of international ministry.* Delores is outspoken, calling it like she sees it, and gets the reader to not only think beyond themselves, but to know why!

Delores served on the International Board of Good Samaritan Ministries for three years, always challenging us to high ideas and effective action! As the founder and CEO of Good Samaritan Ministries for over thirty years, I highly recommend Delores Dillard as an author must read! The challenge will stay with you no matter where you choose to serve.

Bettie P. Mitchell, LPC
Retired Executive Director
Good Samaritan Ministries

WHO IS THE AUTHOR?

Delores Jean Ford grew up in 5th Ward in Houston, Texas. She is the second of five siblings. As far as I can remember she has always been the mature one. She has always been a little different. As a very small child she seemed to know what she wanted and what she was not going to do. Back in the day, that was not always popular or accepted in the adult population. She always had goals. While the rest of us were goofing off or listening to music, she would be somewhere reading. Reading was her favorite pass time.

She began teaching Sunday School at Greater Union Baptist Church, in her teens. She walked to church by herself, Jean and her Bible. Her faith in God was strong. We were blessed to be surrounded by so many Christians. She dreamed of the day that she would be traveling, even though no one in the family had traveled outside of Texas.

She has always spoken her mind, you never had to guess how she felt about anything. Thank God for the heart that he gave her. She sat a great example for the youth in our family, when she decided after raising a family, to go to and graduate from college. She showed them that it is never to late to accomplish anything you really want. She believes that everything happens for a reason and that God is still in control.

Mrs Mary Evans (sister of author)
Retired School Teacher
Houston, Texas

COMMENTS BY OTHER LEADERS

MISSIONARY DELORES DILLARD

I have known Delores for 45 years. She is a woman of God who has hungered and thirsted for righteousness, and has truly walked by faith and not by sight. Her journeys to Africa and other nations have been as an Ambassador for Christ and has represented us sisters well.

Rev. Joyce Smith
Pastor of Community African Methodist Episcopal Church
Vancouver, Washington

I have been blessed to have Delores as my friend since we were very young women, just beginning life as wives and then mothers. She has remained true to her calling and conviction to first of all, God and then by loving people with her acts of love and prayerful devotion as a missionary. I admire her greatly for her faithfulness and determined devotion to serve God with all of her heart, soul and mind.

Sincerely,
Asenath Porter (Daughter of Pastor Taylor, first pastor Vancouver)

Delores is a woman of faith, wisdom and impeccable character. I have accompanied Delores on two mission trips to Africa. Our first trip to Ghana and the second to Rwanda, Burundi and Kenya. The experience was truly a glorious experience and she had prepared me well for the journey.

Pastor Sylvia Jones
Christian Education Pastor
Highland Christian Center
Portland, Oregon

PREFACE

By Rev. Dr. W.G. Hardy Jr.

As an African American growing up in the Pacific Northwest, I recognized early, if I were to be successful I would have to adopt a, "Yes You Can" mentality. I understand more clearly how I was continuously educated and directed toward vacationing in Europe and the islands. However, the third country missions work, I witnessed via media, was performed by well meaning, well intentioned people that generally did not look like the people being ministered too. After several discussions with my friends of diverse backgrounds and ethnicities, I made up my mind, rather than visit the popular advertised vacation places, I would go to Africa.

What I witnessed, to my surprise, was quite a stark contrast to what I had been programmed to believe through television and other mission advertisement. The people of the great continent of Africa were strong resilient, determined and of great faith. What the Africans shared with me caused a significant paradigm shift, a complete different way of my viewing things.

As a visiting African-American, they took me on the inside and shared how much they appreciated the past evangelist and missionaries who had come to build schools, set up missions and address health issues. However, they had been waiting and praying that their family members, who had been separated as a result of the slave trade, would return home and restore what had been severed and broken.

What Missionary Evangelist Delores Dillard shares in book one of "Yes You Can Series" is an answer to the age old prayer of those Africans who have been waiting for the return of the surviving African-Americans. In her book, Delores Dillard expresses the process through which faith grew into reality. She provides, for the reader, lens to see clearly, the calling and provisions of the God of destiny. Delores has been an inspiration to those who know her and know of her. This book is a living testimony that if a person will take the necessary step to start out on the dream God places with in, sure footing will be provided before the next step has to be taken.

Now the just shall live by faith: but if any man draw back, my soul shall have no pleasure in him. Hebrews 10:38 KJV Please sit back and enjoy the journey as your mind's eyes visualize the various episodes that unfold within the pages of this book.

God Bless

Senior Pastor
Highland Christian Center
Portland, Oregon,U.S.A

CONTENTS

MY DEEPEST APPRECIATION TO . . . . .

My husband Kinnard and our sons Karl and Rodney. They released me to go to the nations. None of them have ever traveled with me. But they haven't blocked my way, I am greatful. My family, friends and students for encouraging me to write a book. It has been a labor of love to complete this first book. It would be impossible to name all of these people. But I will name a few of them.

My neighbor and friend, Carole Van Arsdol, who assisted me with the format. My sister, Mary Evans, and friend ,Ann Erickson were two of my readers who gave suggestions on clarity of sentences.

Many have had an impact on my life in various ways. Some of their comments are included in this book. Most of all, I thank God for sending me to the nations. I am glad that he has kept me strong and healthy. I thank him for leading and guiding me every step of the way.

Some of the names and situations have been changed for privacy reasons. But the information for the most part is true and accurate. I didn't know that this trip would give me a thirst for traveling the nations. Since 1983 I have gone to the following nations: United Kingdom, Haiti, St Kitts, Mexico, Israel, Jamaica, Ghana, Liberia, Nigeria, Burundi, Rwanda, Philippines, Kenya and Bermuda.

Each trip has its own story. This is the first of several books about these trips. My desire is to inspire young people to write their own stories. It is also a desire to be an encouragement to older people. As an elder we have so much wisdom to share. We must share our wealth of information with future generations.

I am grateful to all of the people that encouraged me to tell my story. This will also encourage others to follow their dreams. It's not too late to try something new. Life is wonderful, enjoy it to the fullest. If anything about this book touched, inspired or challenged you to believe for the impossible, I thank God. I would love to hear from you. You may contact me at deloresd2003@yahoo.com

Thank you for purchasing this book. May the peace of God rule your heart and mind. This is book 1 of my "Yes You Can Series."

PAPUA, NEW GUINEA 1983

PREPARING FOR THE TRIP

January 1983, New Year's Eve' is a date that I will always remember. It was a time in my life that was the beginning of changing my world view. I was at church for the celebration of the upcoming year. My pastor said the Lord had spoken to him. He said the church would send me to New Guinea. I had told him that this was my desire. The desire started at another church. I had been talking about going to New Guinea for 8 years. I really didn't have much faith that this small church would send me. There were only about 50 people in this congregation. But to my surprise the people embraced the whole idea. A couple sold one of their horses; there were several yard sales.

I asked my husband to release me to go on this trip. I told him I truly believed this was of God. He told me to go if this was God's plan for me. He said he and our two boys would be alright in my absence. This was the first sign of a miracle. My husband releasing me to go wasn't a small thing. Now that I had his blessing, my next step is to talk to the store director of the retail store where I worked. It is July, inventory month, no one is allowed to take vacation time during this period, this includes managers. I am just one of the sales associates. I made an appointment with the director and told him I needed the month of July off for a mission's trip. God gave me favor with the director, he approved my leave. I could start planning for the trip. Many people on my job, family and church members gave me gifts for the New Guineans. The gifts included: school supplies, toiletries, candy and clothes. I had to stop them from giving because I didn't have any more space.

My pastor and the church treasurer were taking care of the arrangement for the plane ticket. I had to get a passport and go to the travel clinic for the necessary immunizations. All of this was new for me. I didn't have anyone to guide me through the necessary steps. No one in my family nor my closest friends had traveled internationally. I had to depend upon the Spirit to lead me. My emotions were very mixed; fear and elation. The weeks passed rapidly as all of the plans lead to the date of departure. My husband was at work when it was time to leave. I sat in my living room and asked God to take care of my family during my absence. I also asked God to protect me and lead me on this trip. There are still many pieces that haven't come together. Every time fear would come upon me, I said God has not given me a spirit of fear. He has given me power, love and a sound mind. I also reminded myself of why I was going. I reflected over the years of desiring to go.

The flight from Portland, Oregon to Hawaii was about five hours. This was my first time seeing the beautiful island. I had three hours to wait for the flight to New Guinea. I walked through the airport and watched the people. This is always a great way to pass the time. After sightseeing in the airport, I found the area where my plane would depart. There were several people going to New Guinea or Australia. A mother and grandmother from California were going to visit their daughter and granddaughter. They gave me some information that was new to me. They said after getting to Port Moresby I would need another ticket to go to Goroka. They said the only way to continue to Goroka after getting to Port Moresby is by a small plane or by boat. This was another opportunity for fear to grip me. I decided again to trust God. The next shocker was we would have to spend the night in a hotel. The next plane wouldn't leave Goroka until the following morning.

These ladies said they had limited funds. It was at this point that I asked if they wanted to share a room after we arrived in Port Moresby. They agreed to this arrangement. After dreaming of going to Papua, New Guinea for so many years the time has finally come. I am on my way to an adventure few people would consider.

ANOTHER SURPRISE

When we landed at the airport in New Guinea, we had to go through customs.

"Where is your visa," the customs agent asked ?

"Visa, what is a visa," I asked?

"Don't you have a visa. How did you arrive in our nation without a visa?"

"I have a ticket, no one ever gave me any information about a visa.

Where can I get a visa?"

"Follow me; I will take you to the officer who can assist you."

I followed him and prayed silently as we went to resolve this unexpected situation. As we walked to the office, I looked at the local people. The people were dark complexion with course short cropped hair. Many of the ladies had babies in a woven colorful carrier that looked like a large purse. The babies were carried on the mother's backs. The mother's were small in statue. They were five feet or shorter. Their clothes were very colorful bright red ,blue, orange and other flashy colors. Many of the locals pointed at me. They communicated in their dialect. They looked perplexed that I wasn't responding to their words.

After a long walk through the airport, the agent said ,"This is the place that you can obtain a visa."

"Thank you, for bringing me to see the officer. I hope this is a short meeting. This has been a long exhausting day."

The officer is sitting behind a small wobbly desk. The desk has several stacks of paper on it. He tells me to sit in the chair in front of the desk. He keeps looking at the paper that the agent gave him. He doesn't make eye contact with me.

" Young lady, why did you come to our nation? Are you here for illegal activities"?

" Sir , I am here by invitation. I want to share the good news with your people. I am a Christian. I came to tell your people about Jesus."

"Why don't you have a visa? It is a crime to enter into this nation without a visa. Are you aware that I could put you in jail for this criminal act?"

"Sir, I wasn't aware that I was going against the law of your land. Would you please forgive me for any wrong that I have done?"

"How long are you planning to stay in our nation?"

"I am planning to stay in New Guinea one month".

" How do I know that you will leave after a month? You might decide to stay longer. If you stay longer you would expect our government to take care of you."

"Sir, I am a married lady with two young boys. My family is waiting for me to return. After a month, I will return home to my family and friends. They are praying for my safe return. I live in a small city in the U.S. This is my first trip out of the U.S. The travel agent wasn't accustomed to booking international flights. The agent didn't know that I needed a visa. So, she couldn't give me guidance."

"Where were you born in the U.S.?

"I was born in Houston, Texas."

"Are there other blacks in America?

"Yes, there are other blacks in America. Typically the southern states have more blacks than in the state of Washington where I currently live. "

"I thought blacks were in Africa. I didn't know they were in America too. Where did they come from?"

I looked at the officer in shock. It is difficult to believe that in 1983, someone would ask this question. I gave him a brief overview of the history of how blacks came to America. This seems to satisfy his curiosity.

After a period that seems like eternity, the man takes my passport and places the visa in it. He stamps the date on it for a one month visit. He looks at me and say, "have a great visit."

Whew, now that ordeal is over. It's time to deal with the next unexpected situation. I was informed that in order to go to Goroka. I would have to purchase another plane ticket or ride on a small boat. The ticket agents were closing for the night. The next time to purchase a ticket would be 7: 30 AM the next morning.

" You will have to purchase your ticket tomorrow. Right now there aren't any vacant seats. But, come back tomorrow to see if there are any cancellations. The plane only leaves when the flight is full. It usually leaves every two weeks. If this one is full you will have to wait two weeks."

The two ladies that I met in Hawaii and I shared a room at the hotel. None of us had much money so this cut expenses. I prayed that God would have a seat on the plane for me the next morning.

I was the first person in line the next morning. The agent asked, "Do you want a window seat."?

I told him it didn't matter as long as I was on that plane. The flight was only an hour. The plane was small , all 24 seats were occupied. God answered prayer again. Because I didn't have enough money to stay two more weeks if this plane was full. I also couldn't pay $85.00 a night for the hotel room.

The plane wasn't leaving until after 10:00 AM. So the other two ladies and I went next door to a small supermarket. We purchased fruit and snacks to eat for breakfast. We took photos of the beautiful scenery. It looked a lot like Hawaii with the beautiful greenery, orchids and palm trees.

The hotel was very nice and modern.

When the plane landed, I still had to pray. I didn't know if anyone would be there to meet me. My original day of arrival was two weeks prior to this date. The previous flight was cancelled because the plane wasn't full. I didn't have a way to inform the missionaries of the change of plans.

As I stepped off the plane, a tall white lady pointed to me. I pointed to her and asked if she was looking for me. She indicated that she was looking for me. I breathed a sigh of relief. I would have really been stranded without this lady. God came through again.

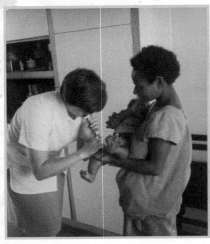 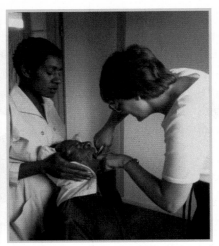

When we were close enough to communicate, I asked "How did you know to come to the airport?"

She said, "When I came to get a friend from the states. The ticket agent informed me that you were on the same flight. He knew your name because he is the one that looked in the system to see if you were on the previous plane."

I said out loud, "Praise the Lord". God is taking care of me. I wasn't trying to put God to the test. I just didn't know proper protocol. I thanked God for his protection. As we traveled the 3 hours by truck, it was like being on a vibrating machine. The roads were the worst that I had ever experienced. This trip in the states would be about 45 minutes. When we arrived at the mission house, it was a relief. The house was raised several feet off of the ground. It was in a woody area on several acres. There weren't any houses close by. The house set on an area that had been cleared.

There was a huge tank on a platform available to catch the rain water. There was a large galvanized tub in a cleared area on the ground on the side of the house. Under the tub was dried grass and wood to start the fire for boiling water.

The mission house was furnished with some American items and local items. It was cozy and inviting. Both of the ladies that I would stay with were single, one was from Illinois the other from Idaho. The other missionaries were a husband and wife with two sons and a third child on the way. All three ladies were nurses. The man was a pastor and a carpenter.

The nurses did everything that remotely fell into the category of medicine- delivering babies, performing operations, pulling teeth. The man, Jeremy, started a carpentry school. The men were taught how to use tools that were totally foreign to them. This would include a saw, hammer, ruler and other strange equipments. They were able to sell these items to earn income.

MEETING THE VILLAGE ELDER

My hostess informed me that the locals were waiting to meet me. They had prayed so many years for me to come. They said we would start visiting the people the next day. The trip from the U.S. to New Guinea was a long one. After eating and getting acquainted, we thanked God for the safe journey. We went to bed and I quickly went to sleep.

The next morning came very quickly. The sun came through the windows quite early. It was very bright and warm. We ate breakfast and left to visit the local people. The first place we went was to the village elder.

His name was Pua. Pua became so excited when he saw me. He started talking so fast. He was speaking in his local dialect. I asked the interpreter what was Pua saying. The interpreter said, Pua said he knew Papa God would send you to us. We prayed and asked God to send you to us to tell us the ways of God.

Pua is the oldest person in the village. They didn't have any records for birth. It was believed that he was 65 years old. This was very old in this culture. Because of tribal wars and diseases, their are few people over 40 years of age. Pua was the first convert in this area. Pua was less than 5 feet.

He wore traditional clothes which consisted of an animal skin to cover the groin area. His chest was bare and he didn't have on any shoes. His hair was matted because of the pig's grease used on it. His teeth were a bright red. I was told the juice from the beetle caused the redness of the teeth. The people chewed the beetle.

Pua said "Before the missionaries came to us. I didn't know anything about God. When my wife died, I ate her body. This was the only way that I knew to keep her with me. Now that I have heard about living forever with God, I know that this isn't right."

Pua invited me into his house. There weren't any windows or light in it.

It was difficult to see because of the darkness. In the middle of the hut, was a kettle over a small fire. The floor of the hut was dirt. The hut was round shaped with a thatched roof and a frame made of red clay. "Why aren't there any windows in the house", I asked?

"We believed that evil spirits come through the windows or where ever there is light. So we kept the house dark to keep evil away", said Pua. Now that we know the Lord, we build our houses so light can enter in. We build them with windows like our American friends."

I thanked Pua for inviting us to his home. When we went out side there was a man leaning over something on the ground. "What's that," I asked.

"It's coffee, said Pastor Jeremy. This is how they dry it before taking it to the market to sell." The coffee was on a piece of cloth. The man was turning the coffee beans so that both sides dried.

We returned to the mission house after a very busy day. Some of the local people were waiting in the yard when we returned. When we went into the house, I asked if we should invite the locals into the house for coffee.

My hostess said, "The people will not come into our house . They have some kind of protocol that prevents them from entering into our house."

I pondered this in my heart. I would find out the reason for this habit.

The next day I had the opportunity to ask Peter, the driver and assistant for the missionaries.

STICKING WITH TRADITION

"Peter, I see that you enter into the mission house. But the other locals stand outside. They won't come into the house. Why do you enter into the house, but the others stand out side?"

Peter looked at me with a quizzical look on his face. He wasn't sure if he should reveal this to me or not. After a few seconds, Peter started to tell me some of the history of his tribe.

His father is one of the local chiefs. Most of his siblings are educated and have college degrees. Because of his status in the village, he is on the same level as the missionaries. He can enter into the house. The other locals aren't educated , therefore, they aren't allowed to enter into the house. This is the protocol according to their tradition. This wasn't anything that the missionaries required.

"What motel did you stay in when you were in Port Moresby," asked Peter?

I responded, "I stayed in a very beautiful place called "The Gateway Motel".

Peter said, "My brother is an architect. He is the one who designed that motel. He is now in Paris designing another motel".

"Peter, that's wonderful. Tell me about your educational system."

"Children go to school if their families can pay the school fees. After they complete primary classes, only the top 10 % continue to high school or college."

"Peter, this means you were one of the students that were in the top of your class. Why are you running errands for the missionaries? You could be working in a professional career. Don't you want to do something else with your life?"

Peter glared at me with a surprised look.

He said, "When I completed high school I worked as an interpreter for the government for several years. When Wally and Phyllis, the first missionaries, came they told me about Jesus. I accepted Jesus as my Lord.

After being set free, all I want to do is serve him. My father wasn't a believer and he couldn't accept that I was a servant for the missionaries. So he demanded that I continue to work for the government. After, he became a believer he told me I was free to do whatever God wanted me to do. So I returned to be the helper for the missionaries. I enjoy this work because I am able to assist people who are here because they love God and want my people to know him. We have a better life because of being taught modern ways to yield more from our labor."

"Peter, that's wonderful that you are working with the missionaries. How long will you continue to do this?"

"I will do this as long as they are here."

Evelyn and Sarah were busy in the clinic the next day. They are training some of the local people how to supervise the clinic. Gloria and Jim look so serious with their gold uniforms. They are administering shots to some of the 100 people that are waiting for service.

I held my breath when I saw the huge opening on a little girl's leg. She was chopping wood and missed the log. Instead of chopping the log, she chopped her leg. When Gloria and Jim cleaned the wound and bandaged the leg, the little girl never moved. Gloria talked to the little girl as Jim gave a shot to prevent infections.

"The child must take these pills everyday twice a day for 10 days," Jim said to the mother. "Keep the bandage dry and change it daily. Do you understand the directions?"

"Yes, I understand when Maco gets up in the morning and before she goes to bed at night she must take one of the pills. Maco was so tired. She was starting to fall asleep.

10

"Maco, God loves you and he is so proud of how you are handling this pain. He knows that you were only trying to help your mother. That's why you were chopping the wood. Would you wait until you are older before chopping wood again," asked Jim?

Maco looked at her mother and quietly whispered, "yes."

Jim helped her get off of the table unto her father's back. This is the mode of transportation to get home.

After all of the patients left the clinic, I asked, "Jim why was such a young child attempting to chop wood. She is too young to even pick up an axe."

Jim looked at me with a look that said I didn't have a clue about this culture. He said, "Delores, in your culture children aren't accustomed to working and helping the family. In our culture everyone is expected to contribute to the needs of the family. A child is expected to watch the younger children. A child as young as five could be watching children a few years younger. You will see many 6 or 7 year old children chopping wood or starting the fire for boiling water."

"Jim, I see what you are saying. Forgive me if I have incorrectly judged your people. I must be reminded that many things are done because it is best for this culture. It doesn't mean that you are wrong or I am right. It only means that things are done differently. Jim, thank you for helping me understand a little more of your culture. I will ponder this information when I see things that are strange to me."

"Good-bye, Evelyn and Sarah I will meet you at the house", said Delores.

The mission house was a short distant from the clinic. Delores was thinking of surprising the missionaries. She would chop the wood and start the fire to boil the water for cooking.

GIVING A HELPING HAND

I gathered some logs and attempted to chop the wood. This was the first time I had ever used an axe. After several minutes, a group of the local people came and watched me trying to cut the log. A little girl about 7 years old took the axe and starting chopping the wood. I was very humbled with this whole event. I wanted to start a fire under the large kettle. I didn't have any matches and was stumped about how to start the fire. The little girl went a few feet and got some dry grass. She rubbed it together until the smoke started coming, then the fire came. I looked in amazement at this event. I didn't know that you could start a fire without matches. The little girl and I couldn't communicate because of the language barrier. I indicated to the little girl that I wanted her to follow me. I went into the house and got a gift for the girl. I gave her a wash cloth, a bar of soap and some lotion. The girl smiled and left to show her gift to some of her friends.

I went to the house and started preparing dinner. The missionaries had a stove similar to the one they had at a home in the U.S. It wasn't difficult cooking on it. Tonight we would have corn beef hash and cabbage. Dessert will be strawberry shortcake. I picked strawberries out of the garden. I made the biscuits needed for the shortcake. The cream from the cows was whipped and placed on the top of the strawberries.

"Whew, what a day", said Evelyn. "We delivered two sets of twins.

Three of our mothers are ready to deliver any time now. They will probably have their babies within the next week. We are on 24 hour call."

"What is that I smell," asked Sarah?

"I couldn't deliver babies or pull teeth. I decided I would come home and prepare dinner. It is my contribution to the ministry," said Delores.

"Thank you, said Sarah and Evelyn in unison. They sat down to eat and rest for a while. At any moment one of the local women could be ready to deliver a baby.

The mission house was quiet and dark. There aren't any street lights.

Everyone had gone to bed and the dogs started barking. We knew someone was coming, and then we heard loud knocking.

"Who's there", asked Sarah?

"It's me," said a male voice. It is George, Mary's husband. Mary is ready to deliver her 8th child.

"Where is Mary now," asked Sarah?

"She is at the clinic," said George.

"Go back to the clinic and stay with her until we arrive, said Sarah. We will be there in a few minutes."

George leaves running to go back to the clinic to be with his wife. It is so dark. I wonder how he knows where to put his feet. At least the missionaries have flashlights. They will go to the clinic in the mission truck.

Sarah and Evelyn prepare to leave the house for the clinic. They take additional medical supplies and lamps in case of any emergency.

"Sarah and Evelyn, I will be praying for you. I pray that everything goes smoothly tonight. May God direct you in whatever is needed."

I prayed while the missionaries were gone. I knew that anything could happen during delivery. "Lord, help Sarah and Evelyn be in tune with you tonight. Help them see any plot of the enemy before he can do any evil. May the mother relax and deliver the baby quickly, in Jesus' name."

After a couple of hours, the missionaries returned home. Sarah said this was one of the easiest births she had ever seen. She thanked me for praying for them. It is quite late now and everyone is ready to go to sleep.

BREAKING TRADITION

The next day is Sunday and I am anticipating preaching through an interpreter for the first time. I have already met many of the members of the community. This will be another highlight of the trip.

We arrived at the church at 10:00 A.M. The church is an a shaped building woven with leaves from the palm trees. The roof is thatched and dry. The floor is the red dirt that is visible all over the nation. There is a concrete platform that is raised off of the floor. A wooden pulpit is on the platform for the minister.

Women wear large beliums on their heads when they come to church.

(Beliums are woven purse like carriers that are used to transport babies, groceries and other items.) They are various colors-solids, multiple colors of red, blue, green and yellow.) On that day the beliums were full of yams, greens and a variety of other food.

As the people filed into the church, I noticed something unusual, at least for me. The women and children sat on the left and the men on the right.

They were very noisy as they greeted one another. Everyone set on the dirt floor, except for guests.

The people had four or five wobbly chairs for the guest. When it was time to minister, Peter informed me he would be one of the interpreters.

There were three interpreters. The people came from several villages. They didn't speak the same dialect.

"My name is Delores I am from the U.S. I am married and have two sons. I thank you for allowing me to share the word of God with you today.

God is not and American God. He is a God for all people no matter where they live or what their nationality is. Many people in the U.S. are praying for you today. They want all of you to know the Lord and experience his unconditional love. God loves you so much that he allowed his only son to die. This son, Jesus, died so that you could have everlasting life. This life is available to anyone that accepts Jesus as their Lord and Savior. I know some of you know the Lord. Others of you are still trying to understand this message. You say this is so different from the god of your forefathers. You don't want to give up the old ways for the new ways. May I ask you a question? If you don't trust this new religion, why do you accept the new medicine?"

"Many of you have come to the clinic for medical assistance. The pills that the missionaries gave you is new. You accept the medicine because of the outcome that you have seen. You have also seen very positive results from many in your village. Pua, will you please stand up? How many of you remember Pua before he became a believer?"

Several heads shook indicating they remembered Pua before he became a Christian. "I was told Pua was a fierce warrior in his earlier days. He didn't have any mercy for any of his enemies. Some people prayed for him to kill them rather than endure the torture."

" When did you notice that Pua's heart had changed toward his enemy?

Was it after he heard the words of God in the Bible? Yes, that's when Pua's heart became soft. He didn't want to kill his enemies any more. He asked his enemies to forgive him. When his enemy needed help building his house, Pua suggested that everyone from this tribe help. This was so strange to the community. Many of you thought Pua had lost his mind. Since Pua is the elder for the village, many of you followed him. Did Pua do this because he was afraid of his enemy? No, he did this because the Bible said to bless your enemy and do good to those who mistreat you. This was such a new experience for you. Some of you had your machetes ready in case the other villagers started to fight. After completing the house, your enemies served yams and greens to you. Many of you became friends with your enemies after that event."

"This is an example of the love of God. He will make you love your enemies. You start to think and do things differently. Now that you have seen several of your own tribes men come to Christ. How many of you want to have a new life with Jesus today? Will everyone close their eyes please?

If you want to accept the Lord Jesus today lift your head and look me in the eyes." Several people looked me in the eyes. "Some of you are looking at me. Are you saying you want to become Christians? If this is the reason that you are looking at me shake your head. Praise God, eight people have indicated they want to become Christians. One of your leaders will talk to you to make sure you understand what you are agreeing too."

After the service, we went outside to eat the lunch that each family brought. There were hooks on the outside of the church building. The beliums were hanging on these hooks. The lunch that each family brought was wrapped in large green elephant leaves. The leaves were used as plates.

All the food was put on these elephant leaves on the ground. Everyone shared their food, which consisted of yams and a vegetable that looked like spinach. Dogs and pigs were running loose and trying to eat some of the food. The local people sat on the ground. They brought the chairs for the visitors to sit in. After lunch we prepared to go back into the church. I needed to ask Peter a question before we entered into the building.

"Peter, should I sit on the side of the room with the ladies? I noticed all of the women sat together apart from the men."

"No, you don't have to sit with the other women. That's the rule we have for our women. But you are American and it's okay."

I was really puzzled by this statement. I decided I'd wait until we returned home to try and get the meaning of this.

The ladies started to pick in one another's head during the service. I didn't have a clue why they were doing this. That would be another question to ask when we returned home. The service lasted about four hours including the time for eating lunch. The people didn't seem to be in a hurry to leave. This was their social event of the week.

"Sarah, why wasn't I required to sit with the other women in church?"

When, I asked Peter, he said I was American as if that really answered my question.

"Delores, the people treat us differently because we are Americans. They are so glad that we are sharing the message of love with them. This is their way to show respect and honor to us."

" I have another question to ask. I saw the ladies picking something out of each others heads. What were they getting out of their hair?

"They were getting fleas out of their hair. Many of the dogs are covered with fleas and the fleas get into the people's hair. So they frequently take turns taking fleas from each others hair."

"I have some kind of bites on my legs and back,are those flea bites,"?

"Yes, the bites are probably flea bites. When we came here we thought the bites were from mosquitoes. But we realized we hadn't seen many mosquitoes. We saw the dogs were very unkept. Many of them were covered with fleas. So we introduced different things to control the fleas.

You will notice the dogs at this compound are healthy and free of fleas. I have something to give you that will eliminate or at least reduce the flea bites."

"Thank you for anything that can assist me with the bites. My legs and back are covered with bites. I'm sure some of the bites will leave permanent marks. The bites itch and it's apparent that I have been scratching when I am asleep. So whatever you have will be helpful."

"Delores, here are some capsules that you must take daily. The ointment must be put on the bites. You will notice a relief from the itching right away.

Keep using the ointment so that none of the bites become infected."

"Thank you, for your help, it's good that I am living with a medical provider".

"Delores, we will be going to weigh new infants and check on the status of new mothers tomorrow. This is a new village that was not open to the gospel in previous years. Because of the medical services that we provide, they allow us to present the gospel. Would you like to go with us to assist us and tell a Bible story to the children?"

"Yes, I look forward to meeting the people and presenting the gospel to the children. Is there a particular story that you have in mind?"

"It doesn't matter which story you tell. They aren't familiar with the Bible so it will be new to them. Whatever you tell make it active and include the children in the presentation. They love to sing and be involved in whatever is done."

"I have some puppets of different Bible characters and animals. I will take these with me. I will ask some of the children to help me tell the story.

This will be fun for all of us. What time will we be leaving? How long will it take us to get there?"

"We will be leaving at 9:00 A.M. It takes one hour to get to this village, if it doesn't rain. It can take two hours or longer if it rains. Remember, the conditions of the roads don't allow us to go fast."

I went to my room and thanked God for using me in the service today.

This was my first time preaching in a foreign land and God allowed me to see some come to him. "God I thank you for those who accepted you today.

I ask that each of those who received you know the depth of your love.

They will know that they are free from the old ways and can walk without fear. Help them to know they are never along. Lord, protect the word that they heard, let it go deep into their heart. May this whole nation come to know you, as they see the peace and joy in the lives of these new believers, in Jesus' name."

GOING TO A NEW VILLAGE

I awaken to the smell of coffee. It was time to get up and get ready for the new venture. I took a shower and dressed for the day. Sarah and Evelyn were already dressed. The four ladies sat down to a breakfast of cereal, juice and coffee.

Velma, the other visitor from the U.S., decided she would join us today.

She said, "I can't preach in a church, but I can assist you with the story for the children."

"That's great I can use your help. None of us have any idea how many children we will have. I know in the states all children like to sing and watch a puppet show. I think this is something that will draw many children. Let's take some balls and balloons with us. I have some candy to give also."

Evelyn and Sarah laughed at Velma and I. Evelyn said," it seems as though you ladies are planning for quite a production with the children. I'm not sure who will enjoy this event the most, you or the children."

The ladies loaded all of the medical supplies and toys into the truck.

Besides the four ladies three of the local people were joining them. It's not the custom to go anywhere with room left in a moving vehicle. The people will sit on one another's lap to get into the vehicle. Frequently, chickens, dogs and pigs will also be in the vehicle. Today it was just people and equipment. We are also blessed to have a sunny day for the hour-long trip.

When we arrive at the village, there was a line already formed. Word had spread that medical care would be provided. There were 10 mothers and babies and 15 children waiting for us. The equipment was taken out of the truck and the nurse's set up their station. The nurse's assistance gave cards to the mothers. They gave blue cards for the infant boys and pink for the girls. They wrote the mother's name, child's name and date of birth on each card.

Evelyn and Sarah hung a scale upon a tree. The scale is the kind that is used in the states to weigh vegetables on. The mother brought the infant wrapped in a blanket. The assistant gave the card to Evelyn to record the weight of the baby. Sarah unwrapped the infant and told Evelyn the weight.

Velma and I decided to have a puppet show about the story of Jonah.

George and Gloria, two of the children from the community, came to assist us. The other children

in the community were curious about what we were doing. George decided he would be the large fish. He made a loud noise when he swallowed Jonah. When the fish was releasing Jonah, George had quite a performance. The children jumped up and down and laughed. This encouraged George to continue with his actions. After the production, we gave the children the balloons, balls and candy.

Velma continued to play with the children. I went to assist the nurses.

There was still a line of those who were waiting for service. The word had passed in the village that the nurses were present. So other women came to get their babies weighted. I took one baby named Chester and unwrapped him to put on the scale. When I unwrapped Chester, I shouted to Sarah, "this isn't a boy this is a girl." We assumed Chester was a boy. We don't know where they heard this name. We laughed and I said," I wouldn't name a boy Chester and certainly wouldn't put this name on a girl."

Sarah said," I doubt that any of these people have ever seen the American television show Gun Smoke. There's a character on it by the name of Chester. It would be interesting to find out where they heard the name Chester. I would hate to be a girl with the name Chester."

After three hours, and 25 babies, the team was on there way home. It was a long hot ride back home. Everyone was tired but fulfilled with the out come of the day. We were able to weigh 25 babies, give medical advice to the mother's and have a puppet show for 50 children.

After dinner the four ladies reflected on the events of the day. Everyone laughed at the discovery of Chester being a girl.

DESIRE TO TRAVEL

"Delores, how did you happen to come to New Guinea, asked Velma?

This isn't the usual place to come for a vacation. Tell us your story."

"Well, it started when I was a little girl. My mother was a member of the women's missionary group in our local church. The church was Union Missionary Baptist Church in Houston, Texas. This was before integration so it was rare to see anyone that wasn't African American in our mist.

When the women got together for their regular meetings they would read the Bible and talk about missionaries. I heard the stories and fantasized about being a missionary in far away places. I had never seen or talked to a missionary. But, God was preparing my heart for the future."

"In 1964, I moved to Vancouver, Washington to live with my father. I had graduated from high school in 1962 and was ready for a change. I accepted the Lord at 6 years of age. I came from a family of church goes.

When I came to Vancouver, I had many culture shocks. The first one was, you could go for days and not see another African American. The second shock was there weren't any African American churches in Vancouver. So these two factors lead me to a very unfamiliar path—a path that I hadn't ever thought of nor considered."

"Tell us what your feeling were regarding the city being so predominately white. Did you feel uncomfortable? Were you afraid," asked Velma.

"I didn't feel afraid as much as I felt uncomfortable. In Houston, you worked for or with whites, but you didn't go to school or church with them.

You didn't have a friendship or relationship with them. So coming to Vancouver was a real shock. You would have to associate with whites in order to survive. The percentage of African Americans is about 2%. I knew that I wanted to go to church. There weren't any African American churches in Vancouver. There were some in Portland, Oregon. But, I didn't know the area and I didn't have transportation. So the little church in the neighborhood would have to do. I didn't have any other choice."

"The neighborhood church was Open Bible Community Church. The pastor was O.I. Taylor and his wife Wilehemina. He was Italian and she was German. They welcomed me and made me feel accepted. They taught me the word of God and how to live as a believer. The love that they gave me was genuine. It was at this church that I saw my first missionaries. When the missionaries came to the states, they came to various churches to give their reports. Sometimes we invited them to our house for dinner. Weather they were at my house or at church, I listened and asked questions."

When the monthly periodicals from the national headquarters came, I eagerly read the reports of the missionaries. In 1973 the heat of racism was going on in our nation. I thought I would write an article to give my feeling on some of the racial issues. This article appeared in "The Messenger." This magazine went to all of the places that there were members of the organization. One night I came to Bible study and the pastor said, "Delores you have a letter from New Guinea."

"I didn't have a clue where New Guinea was. I knew Guinea was in Africa. But didn't know where New Guinea was located. I waited to read the letter when I returned home. The letter was from the Lee's, some missionaries, in Papua, New Guinea. They read the article and showed my picture to the local people. The locals were shocked to see that I was black like them. They started praying for papa God to send me to teach the word of God to them."

"What did you think when you read the letter? Did you decide you want to come to New Guinea then or was it later?"

"I decided then I wanted to come." I was so excited I asked my husband didn't he want to come to New Guinea with me. He gave me a strange look and said I could go if I wanted to but, he and our boys would stay home.

After almost 15 years, I started attending another church. I had been gone from Open Bible Church for 8 years. I hadn't made it to New Guinea, yet. But I told people at the new church about my desire. On New Years Eve 1983, Pastor Mike Miller said God had just spoken to him. He said New Covenant Fellowship Church would send me to New Guinea.

" I really didn't believe this church would send me anywhere. There were only about 50 people in that church. It was not a wealthy or upscale church. The people got busy with yard sales and a couple sold one of their horses. So the word was spoken January 1983 that I would be sent to New Guinea. July 1983, I was heading to New Guinea on a one way ticket. The ticket was one way because that was the amount the church was able to raise. The pastor said they would purchase the return ticket within the 30 days for my flight home."

"You mean to tell me your husband allowed you to come with a one way ticket,"? asked Velma.

"My husband didn't know it was a one way ticket. I knew he wouldn't allow me to come if he knew, so I kept that to myself. When I received the ticket, I said to the Lord. It is up to you to get me home. I am trusting you in this. I believe you are sending me so the responsibility is yours to bring me home. I didn't tell my family or friends. I had to stand in faith and many times talking will bring fear to you. That's a summary of how I came to New Guinea."

"What will your family and friends say when you return home? After you tell them that the ticket was one way", asked Sarah?

"Most of my friends and family will be upset when they hear the one way ticket story. But they can't do anything after the fact."

" How did this trip affect your faith walk. Did it help you to trust God more or less," asked Sarah?

"It definitely helped me have more faith and trust in God. I knew that I couldn't allow my faith to waver. Faith in God was all that I had. There wasn't anyone or anything else that I could trust."

"In order to have faith for healing or financial blessing, you have to be tested. It's in the testing you learn how to stand. I would never know if God could provide finances for me if I hadn't been in need. Now, that God has brought me here. I also believe he will take me home at the appointed time."

"Tomorrow we will have another busy day. We will visit a high school.

The children are excited to have an African American visitor. Delores, you will be the first African American that any of the people have met. The children and staff have lots of questions", said Evelyn.

"I am also looking forward to interacting with the students and staff.

Hopefully, I will have the answers to their questions.

VISITING A HIGH SCHOOL

After a restless night, it was finally time to get dressed for the trip. We ate breakfast and went to visit the high school. Upon our arrival at the school, I noticed the beautiful plants. It looked like a tropical paradise.

There were various palm trees and different color orchids: yellow, white, red and purple. The school building was very modest. It was located on a small plot of cleared land. When we came on the property, several of the students started running toward the truck.

"Move out of the way," screamed the instructor. There was the feeling of excitement in the air. The students surrounded the truck making getting out difficult. I had a new understanding of the scripture that said the crowds pressed to get to Jesus. The head master of the school parted the crowd as if it was the Red Sea. We walked through the middle of the students. Some were on both sides of us. They didn't have on any special clothing or uniforms. There were about 350 boys and girls.

"Welcome to our school, said the head master. We are honored to have you visit us. As you can see, the students are extremely happy that you are here. One of our most brilliant students will officially welcome you. James, please come and greet our visitors."

"Good afternoon ladies and gentlemen my name is James. The student body and staff thank you for coming to our school today. We feel special that you have come to visit us. As a member of the student leaders, we welcome you and hope that you will enjoy your visit. We have prepared a short program in your honor."

The students sang a song in their dialect and then sang it in English. The words of the song were very touching. They sang friends are special.

Friends are more valuable than money or jewels. You have to be a good friend to have good friends. After the song, another student quoted a poem that she had written. We thanked the students for their song and poem. We asked if any of them had any questions. It seems as though they were waiting for their opportunity to ask questions.

"Where do you live in the U.S", asked one girl named Marie?

"I live in the state of Washington in the Pacific Northwest," I said.

"Washington, isn't that where the president lives in the White House"?

"No, the White House and the president are on the east coast, that's the

District of Columbia. I live on the west coast."

"How many blacks are there in the U.S"?

"There are about 12% blacks in America. In the state of Washington, where I live, blacks represent 2% of the population.

Most blacks live in southern states. This is due to slavery. When blacks were brought to the U.S. from Africa. They were taken to the southern states to farm the crops. The weather is much warmer in the south.

Therefore, it was a good place to grow cotton and tobacco and other crops.

The southern states climate was also more adaptable for the slaves because it's similar to climate, in Africa. After slavery was abolished most of the blacks remained in the southern states."

"You say you are African American. If you are African why isn't your skin dark like the Africans"?

"When the slaves were owned by the whites, the owners had complete control. The slave owners fathered many children from the slaves.

Therefore, African Americans complexion range from fair to mahogony.

When a baby is born, it's always a mystery of the hue of the child.

Sometimes the child will be as white as the slave owner or as chocolate as a great great grandparent. If a family has six children, it's possible that each child is a different shade of brown."

"During slavery the lighter skinned slaves were given different privileges than the darker ones. The lighter skinned would usually be given chores in the house, such as a cook, seamstress, nanny or housekeeper. The darker ones worked in the cotton fields and did other strenuous labor. This often caused families to be more divided. "

"Delores, thank you for giving us some African American history.

Would you please take a photo with us", asked the head master? This is an important historical occasion for us."

"I would be honored to take a photo with you and your students. This is also an important occasion for me. I will have the opportunity to show the photos to many people. I will be able to tell them about you."

After, taking the photos we thanked the staff and students and said good- bye. It was a great time with all of them.

We piled into the truck. There were a couple of locals that joined us. I sat in the front with the driver. I felt some one touching my head and rubbing my arms. Why are they touching my head and arms?

Peter responded, "it is difficult for the people to believe you are real.

Your skin and hair is similar to ours. But you are also very different than us in so many ways"

"Peter, the biggest difference is the language. The other things are more alike than different. If I spoke your dialect, you wouldn't think of me as different, would you?

"Well there is another major difference that the community is talking about," responded Peter.

"What's that Peter"?

"Well, this is the first time that we have seen a black person and a white living in the same house. Is this common in the U.S?

"Peter, this is still not common in many places in the U.S. For instance, in Texas where I was raised, it wouldn't be seen. But, in Washington where I live now, it is a little more acceptable. But you don't see the mixing of the nationalities in churches either. Most of the blacks go to predominately African American churches. And the same is true with the whites; they usually go to churches that are mostly filled with whites."

" I don't understand. When the missionaries came they told us God loves all of us the same. If this is true, why are the races separated even in the church", asked Peter?

"Peter, this is a little hard to explain. But I will attempt to answer that question. During slavery most of the whites didn't allow the blacks to enter their churches. A few denominations allowed the blacks to come to their churches if they set apart from the rest of the congregation. So all of these years after slavery, for the most part, the separation continues. There is such a vast difference in the preaching and singing style of the nationalities, neither race feels comfortable with the other's church service. Today, it's not a matter of preventing the blacks from going to a predominately white church. Most blacks don't want to attend their churches."

The days have gone very fast. We went to a local market today. Most of the products come from Australia. The products are very similar to the ones in the states. Some of the names are the same. There are several open markets where the locals sell their goods. We stepped over half of a hog that had been slaughtered and ready to be sold. There wasn't any concern that it was on the concrete and wasn't on ice. The merchant had a woven hand fan to keep the flies in control. This is the way life is. No one is in a rush and there's no sign of anxiety about food poisoning.

FAREWELL PARTY

The local people are preparing a going away party for me tomorrow. I will be leaving to go home the following day. Several have expressed how much they loved me and don't want me to leave. They are busy getting the food for the big event. The people are preparing everything. It is their idea not—the missionaries. They are preparing everything the traditional way.

Today is Thursday, the day of the farewell party. The people are up very early preparing the food. They dug a hole in the ground about three feet deep. They lined this hole with bricks made from the red clay. They started a fire on the bricks. Next they wrapped some pork in the green plant, that looks like an elephant ear. This was tied with a piece of string. The bundles of pork and vegetables are placed on the hot bricks. Then a mound is made over this hole. In the center of the mound is a hole.

"Belay, what are you going to do with the bamboo stick," I asked?

He said, "Wait you will see." Belay cut an eight feet bamboo stick. He cleans the inside of the pole and leaves the bottom part in tack. Then he fills the bamboo with water. After filling the

bamboo, he pours the water over the pork and vegetables. This results in an immediate gush of steam. Leaves are laid over the hole in the mound. This is done to hold the steam in the mound, while the meal is cooking.

After getting the food in the "oven", William said, "we can go away until time for the celebration. When we are ready for the party, the food will be ready."

We left the food to cook and went to do some of the daily chores at home. I had just returned into the house, when I heard a knock on the door.

It was Peter. He said, "I have a gift for you". He gave me this old heavy rock. I thanked him for the rock.

"Do you know why this rock is special, "he asked?

"No, I'm sorry I don't know why this rock is special".

"Look at the shape of the rock. What does it look like to you "?

"Oh, I see the rock is the shape of an axe".

"Yes, that's right. This is what we used to chop wood for hundreds of years. When the missionaries came they showed us how to put a handle on the rock. This made life a lot easier for us. This rock was given to me by my grandfather. It has been in our family for several generations. It is very special to me. I want you to have it. I don't ever want you to forget us."

"Peter, I am so blessed that you would give me such a special gift. Are you sure you want to give me something that is so much a part of your family?"

"Yes, you are a friend to me and my people. You deserve to have something that is meaningful to us. This rock represents the old life before Christ. Now, we have another way to chop wood. It is a part of the new life in Christ. The old life is gone. A new life has begun. I thank you for coming to share with us. Our lives are forever changed because of your visit. I will see you later at the party. I have to go and take care of some other details."

"Peter, thank you again for this significant gift. I will always cherish it.

It will always remind me of this first trip in another nation. Good-bye, I will see you later"

I wrote in my journal the last events. I examined the rock after Peter left.

It's hard to imagine that it was used to chop wood. This was a back breaking job. It must have taken all day to chop wood for cooking and heat. I bet this was a job that the women and children had to do. I reflected over the weeks in this nation. The men usually have bow and arrows with them. But I don't recall seeing any animals that were brought home for dinner. I wondered if they just carried the bow for protection as they did in the old days. This will be a question to ask the group at the party. I felt tired all of a sudden. I will take a short nap and be rested for the party.

"Delores, Delores, everyone is waiting for you. They are ready to start the party," said Evelyn.

"Oh, I wasn't planning to sleep for more than a few minutes. I will wash my face and change clothes. I will be there soon. I changed with rapid speed and went to the party.

The scene was different than any party that I have seen in the states. In the center of the cleared area was the food that had been "barbequing."

Around the mound were the Americans and locals. There were four chairs on the side for the American ladies. The chairs didn't look very stable.

"Delores, we want you to sit in this chair", said Peter.

"Peter, I can sit on the ground with the others."

"No, you must sit here this is the seat of honor," said Peter.

I reluctantly sat in the chair. I didn't move around too much for fear that the chair would collapse.

A group of the ladies came in a line singing a song in their dialect. Peter interpreted the words. They sang, Papa God answered our prayers. We asked him to send Delores to us. We wanted to hear more of His word. God loves us and granted us our request. We praise and thank God for this answer.

Pua, the oldest elder of the community, blessed the food as we prepared to eat. The usual dogs, chickens and pigs were running loose in the area.

The food was placed on the green elephant leaf plants. These were our "plates." Marie handed my plate to me. Those who were sitting on the ground, had to protect their food from the animals.

I looked up to see a group of the locals staring at me. I smiled at them and was curious why they were watching me. After several minutes, I asked Evelyn did she know why the people were watching me so intensely.

Evelyn said "visitors from the US. came to visit three months ago. When they were preparing to leave, the locals prepared a party for them. When it was time to eat the meal, the couple left the party. They said they didn't see how we could eat the food. They said the people were dirty and the food wasn't sanitary. The local people were so hurt and puzzled by this response.

So, they are waiting to see if you will respond in the same manner."

I ate the first serving of greens, yams and pork. "This is very tasty. May I have some more please"? Marie and the other locals smiled and rushed to get more food for me. After the delicious meal, I thanked everyone for the wonderful visit to Papua, New Guinea. I told them I would share my experience with many people. I asked if I could pray for them before I leave.

Their response was in the affirmative. I asked God to assist them as more people are coming to their nation. I asked God to protect the word of God that they have heard.

The next day was filled with mixed emotions as I left the mission house to go to the airport. Many of the local people were standing outside to say their last good-bye. Several of them had tears rolling down their cheeks.

They were feeling some of the emotions that I felt. I hugged them and went to sit in the truck. This is my final day in Papua, New Guinea I am on my way home.

Printed in the United States
By Bookmasters